STAR WARS®

THE CLONE WARS™

BOUNTY HUNTER: BOBA FETT

adapted by Jason Fry
illustrated by Wayne Lo

Grosset & Dunlap
An Imprint of Penguin Group (USA) Inc.

LucasBooks

GROSSET & DUNLAP
Published by the Penguin Group
Penguin Group (USA) Inc., 375 Hudson Street, New York, New York 10014, USA
Penguin Group (Canada), 90 Eglinton Avenue East, Suite 700,
Toronto, Ontario M4P 2Y3, Canada
(a division of Pearson Penguin Canada Inc.)
Penguin Books Ltd., 80 Strand, London WC2R 0RL, England
Penguin Group Ireland, 25 St. Stephen's Green, Dublin 2, Ireland
(a division of Penguin Books Ltd.)
Penguin Group (Australia), 250 Camberwell Road, Camberwell,
Victoria 3124, Australia
(a division of Pearson Australia Group Pty. Ltd.)
Penguin Books India Pvt. Ltd., 11 Community Centre, Panchsheel Park,
New Delhi—110 017, India
Penguin Group (NZ), 67 Apollo Drive, Rosedale, North Shore 0632, New Zealand
(a division of Pearson New Zealand Ltd.)
Penguin Books (South Africa) (Pty.) Ltd., 24 Sturdee Avenue,
Rosebank, Johannesburg 2196, South Africa
Penguin Books Ltd., Registered Offices:
80 Strand, London WC2R 0RL, England

This book is published in partnership with LucasBooks, a division of Lucasfilm Ltd.

Library of Congress Control Number: 2009044187

ISBN 978-0-448-45413-9   10 9 8 7 6 5 4 3 2 1

A Republic frigate roared across the black of space, carrying a brigade of eleven-year-old clone cadets under the watchful eye of Clone Sergeant Crasher.

"War does not come with a guarantee," Crasher said to the cadets. "But men, I guarantee you this: Every member of this Clone Youth Brigade will have his moment. And it is that moment when you will no longer be a cadet—you will be a soldier."

Cadet Jax looked through the bridge's viewports at a point of light in the distance. *There's the Jedi cruiser*, he thought, trying to keep the excitement from showing on his face.

Crasher left the bridge and the cadets broke off into groups. All except for one, Jax noticed. One cadet, his hair longer than the regulation length, stood alone . . . until cadets Whiplash and Hotshot caught sight of him.

"Who's the new guy with the long hair?" Jax heard Hotshot say to Whiplash.

"Some last-minute replacement," Whiplash replied.

"Hey. What outfit you from?" Whiplash asked the new cadet.

"322nd," the cadet replied.

"I heard they had their tour," Hotshot said.

"I—I couldn't make it. Broken arm," the cadet added.

"A real trooper could lose an arm and still report for duty," Hotshot said with a sneer.

"What are you, soft?" added Whiplash.

That's enough, Jax decided, stepping into the group.

"C'mon, Whip," Hotshot said casually as he saw Jax heading their way. "Air's getting stale around here."

Jax watched them go, then turned to the new cadet.

"What's your name?" He asked.

"I'm Lucky," he said. "Thanks, but I can handle myself."

"Sure, but a trooper's only as strong as the trooper beside him," Jax said. "We're all in it together, right?"

Lucky gave him a small smile. "Right."

Just then the Jedi cruiser passed overhead, ready for the smaller frigate to dock.

Crasher marched the cadets out of the frigate and into the cruiser's docking bay, where a line of clone troopers stood waiting. Veterans of the war against the Separatists, their armor was scarred and stained by battles, as were the white helmets they cradled in their arms.

Marching beside Lucky, Jax saw that most of the cadets stared at the older clones with fear and awe. But Lucky's eyes were turned away, as if he didn't want to look.

"Don't be nervous," Jax said. "Only thing between us and them is experience. It's not like they're Jedi."

As he said that, a door whooshed open and two tall figures exited.

"Welcome aboard the *Endurance*," the older Jedi said. "I am Mace Windu."

"Anakin Skywalker," the younger Jedi said. "Today you'll see how a real, working Jedi cruiser operates. And you'll have the chance to serve right alongside two Jedi Knights."

That was too much for even well-trained cadets to resist. The young clones began to chatter excitedly, stopping only when a clone trooper marched up to the two Jedi.

"Generals," the trooper said to the Jedi. "New orders from General Kenobi await you in the war room. Immediately."

The two Jedi exited the docking bay.

Later, from the cruiser's gunnery room, the cadets watched as a laser blast from the *Endurance* blew apart a metal ball spiraling through the emptiness of space.

Admiral Kilian nodded in approval at Gunnery Sergeant Fury, who was seated at the blaster cannon's controls. The admiral was squat and bald, but the cadets still felt nervous under his gaze. Aboard the *Endurance*, his word was law.

"Looks easy, doesn't it?" Fury asked the cadets. "Well, looks can be deceiving. There's nothing more dangerous in all of space than a moving target."

"What do you use for targets, sir?" asked Cadet Jax.

"Malfunctioning droids," Fury said. That brought a frightened chirp from R2-D2, who was watching the practice. Fury laughed.

Kilian ignored the sergeant. "Mechanical skeet packed with explosives," he said. "Now, this is my ship and my rules. I do not allow tourists on board. Only soldiers. Time for target practice."

He pointed at Jax. "You there . . . take the gun."

Jax sat in the gunner's seat and nodded as a skeet flashed across space. The other cadets rushed to the observation port. Jax took aim and fired. A near miss! The cadets groaned.

"Near miss is still a miss, kid," Fury said.

"The sergeant's right," Kilian agreed. "Training is no match for experience. And it's the one thing none of you have."

The admiral sensed one of the cadets glaring at him. It was Lucky. He returned the youth's gaze, a hint of a smile on his face.

"You're next," he said.

Jax climbed down from the cannon and Lucky took his place in the gunner's seat. Before he could get set, another skeet hurtled across the starfield.

Lucky calmly closed one eye and squeezed the trigger.

BOOM! Direct hit! The cadets cheered.

"I see why they call you Lucky," Fury said.

Three more skeets darted across space, crisscrossing in a deadly pattern. Lucky calmly fired—once, twice, and then a third time—blasting the skeets to bits. The other cadets cheered.

"All right, all right," Crasher said. "Cut the chatter, cadets. We're due on Observation Deck 13. Fall out!"

As they marched out, Kilian nodded proudly at Lucky.

"Now that's a cadet to watch," he said.

CHAPTER 2

Later, the cadets were marched around the cruiser. As Crasher quizzed them about the ship's systems, Lucky quietly slipped away.

Once alone, he popped a small comlink into his ear.

"Boba, is that you?" asked a harsh voice.

"It is," replied Lucky as a holographic map of the cruiser appeared in his hand. "Received transmission. Boba out."

The young cadet known as Lucky was none other than Boba Fett!

Boba crept through the corridors, avoiding the crew members as they went about their business. He was nearing his target when two troopers came around a corner and almost bumped into him. Boba shut off the hologram and stared up at the clones.

"Hey, what are you doing here?" one demanded.

"Communiqué, sir, eyes only," Boba said. "I've been dispatched to General Windu's quarters. There's no problem, sir."

The clones stared at him.

"Oh, there is a problem," one of the clone troopers said. "You're lying."

Boba felt his heart jump and the blood pounding in his head. *Remain calm*, he thought to himself. *That's what Dad would have done.*

"Admit it," the clone said. "You're lost."

"Come on, cut the kid a break," the other trooper said, then pointed. "Windu's quarters are that way, shiny."

"Yes, sir," Boba said. "Thank you, sir!"

Once inside Mace's cabin, Boba reached beneath his belt and retrieved a flat, rectangular detonator. He activated the device and its readout began to glow. Boba smiled. The countdown had begun.

As Boba Fett fled the cabin, he almost immediately ran into Mace Windu.

"Eyes on where you're headed," the Jedi said sharply, thinking Boba was a clone cadet.

Mace Windu had killed his father, bounty hunter Jango Fett, in the arena on Geonosis— the same Jango Fett who had been cloned to make an army for the Republic. The clone troopers that fought for the Republic were altered so that they aged at an accelerated rate. But Boba hadn't been altered, and Jango had raised him as his son.

"Yes, sir," Boba replied. "Sorry, sir."

Mace could sense something. A ripple in the Force. Something wasn't right. But then many things were wrong in the galaxy, and he was tired.

The cadet hurried away and Mace continued toward his cabin, only to be stopped by a clone trooper.

"Sir," the trooper said. "General Skywalker requests your presence on the bridge."

Mace handed the clone a stack of data disks.

"No rest for the weary," he said. "Put these inside my quarters, would you?"

Mace turned to leave as the clone reached for the door controls.

The cadets felt an explosion shake the Jedi cruiser and looked around in confusion as the emergency lighting switched on and alarms began to blare.

"This doesn't look like a drill," Jax told Boba, who'd lived up to his name of "Lucky" by reappearing before Sergeant Crasher realized he was lost.

"No time for chatter," Crasher ordered. "There's been an explosion."

A clone trooper rushed up to Crasher.

"Ship's undamaged, one man down," the trooper reported. "General Windu's quarters got hit, but he survived."

Boba gasped.

Anakin and Mace surveyed the charred remains of Mace's cabin.

"This was no accident," Anakin said.

Mace looked even more grim than usual. "Agreed."

"Ship's navigation is nearby," Anakin noted.

Mace raised his comlink. "Admiral, has the navigation been damaged?"

"Hobbled, not destroyed," Admiral Kilian said. "Systems are repairable. I've ordered shutdown of all engines until we're fully operational. We'll hold orbit over Vanqor."

"Any sign of a Separatist attack?" Anakin asked.

"None, but we'll keep scanning," Kilian said. "Until we get navigation back, the *Endurance* is a fat and easy target."

"If navigation wasn't the target," Anakin said, "then your quarters was."

Within minutes, the Jedi had gathered a squad of clone troopers.

"We have a killer on board this ship and we are locked in dead space," Mace said.

"And so is our assassin," Anakin added. "We'll form an unbroken line of troopers and scour the ship from bow to stern, checking every corridor, bulkhead, and storage unit."

"I want him alive," Mace said.

CHAPTER 3

It had been harder for Boba to slip away a second time, but he was once again creeping through the *Endurance*'s corridors.

"Watcher, this is Boba," he whispered into his comlink. "It's a miss. Repeat, miss. What should I do?"

"Head to the reactor," came the reply. "Blow the core."

"But the crew! It isn't about them, just Mace!" Boba replied.

"If you want Windu dead," the voice said, "do as I say!"

Boba opened a door and entered the main reactor room. The machinery hummed with energy.

"Hey, you there!" a clone trooper called out. "Come here!"

"I got lost, sir," Boba said. "I just . . . I'll return to my brigade."

"Not alone you won't," the trooper replied. "Emergency protocol's in effect. I'm calling a trooper to escort you out of here."

Boba pointed to the soldier's blaster.

"Is that a DC-15A?" he asked.

The clone handed the blaster to Boba.

"Here," he said. "Keep the safety on."

Boba stared at the blaster. The clone trooper turned and activated his comlink. Boba raised the blaster like a club and brought it down on the trooper's helmet. But the blow just glanced off. The trooper turned, startled, and Boba swung the blaster harder this time. The trooper fell heavily and the impact knocked off his helmet, revealing his face.

Boba's eyes went wide as he looked at the same face as his father's.

"What are you doing?" the clone demanded. "We're brothers! Don't shoot!"

"You're not my brother," Boba said. "Don't worry, I won't kill you."

The trooper swiped at Boba's feet, knocking him to the deck. Boba jumped up again, switched the blaster's safety off, and fired a stun bolt into the trooper's chest. As he crumpled to the floor, his comlink blared to life.

"CT-1477, report in! CT-1477, why have you broken—"

Boba switched it off, thinking of Geonosis, where he'd knelt with his father's Mandalorian helmet, then buried his body in the red sands. That was where he'd been left alone.

Suddenly he started smashing the reactor controls with the blaster and spinning knobs and dials randomly. When the alarms began whooping, he turned and ran from the room.

Admiral Kilian joined Anakin, Mace, and a line of clone troopers searching the corridors.

"Our sweep has now covered over half the ship, Admiral," Anakin said.

Kilian narrowed his eyes and looked around. "The more ground we cover, the less there is in which to hide."

BOOM! Another explosion rocked the ship, far bigger than the first one.

Clones and bits of shredded metal were sucked through a gaping hole and into deep space. The *Endurance*, broken, began to drift.

Now there was no need for Boba Fett to hide at all. With the *Endurance*'s reactor core doomed and the distress beacon activated, the crew was too busy to worry about lost cadets. Boba found the other clones in the chaos of the escape pod bay.

"Lucky!" Crasher barked. "Stay with the group!"

"Yes, sir," Boba said meekly.

Crasher ushered the cadets to a row of escape pods. Boba found himself grouped with Jax, Whiplash, and Hotshot. They scrambled into their pod; Crasher looked at them through the hatch.

"This is the moment, men," he said. "Make it yours."

The pod shot into space. Boba stared out at the stricken cruiser. Then he noticed Jax was frantically pawing at the controls.

"The pod's malfunctioned!" he cried.

The pod hurtled past the others, headed for deep space.

On the bridge of the cruiser, Anakin and Mace stood with Admiral Kilian, watching the planet Vanqor growing ominously on the main viewing screen. Commander Ponds struggled with the controls. Small bursts of flame erupted from overloaded systems. R2-D2 used his built-in extinguisher to douse one of the eruptions.

"Admiral," Mace said to Kilian. "You must abandon ship."

"Not a chance," he replied.

"But, sir," Anakin said. "With respect, that's an order."

"It may be your command, General," the admiral replied, "but it's my ship."

"We don't have time for that kind of sentiment," Anakin protested.

"It's not sentiment," Kilian replied firmly. "An admiral must go down with his ship. I don't expect you to understand it, Jedi."

CHAPTER 4

Aboard the escape pod, Jax was trying to bring the control systems back to life.

"Navigation's shot," he said.

"Can we steer?" Whiplash asked.

"No," Jax responded.

"How about fuel?" Hotshot asked.

"No need," Jax added. "We're deadweight."

"So what do we do?" Hotshot asked.

Jax stared at him. "Our jobs."

A bright light passed over the pod, and the clones heard the clunk of another ship docking with their lifeboat.

"Rescue ship?" Whiplash asked hopefully.

"It's too early," Jax said, puzzled.

The pod's hatch opened. On the other side stood a long-limbed woman with bone white skin. Behind her was a green-skinned Trandoshan.

"Well, what do we have here?" the woman asked in a harsh voice. "You boys look lost. Congratulations, Boba. Job well done."

"His name's not Boba," Jax protested. "He's Lucky."

"Lucky?" she repeated, her smile cruel. "That's a good one."

Jax looked from Boba to the pale woman and the Trandoshan.

"You're with her?" he asked.

Boba didn't answer.

"I wasn't expecting you to bring friends along," the woman said.

"I couldn't help it, Aurra," Boba said. "What are you going to do with them?"

"What do you think?" Aurra asked.

"Let them go," Boba said.

"They're living witnesses, honey," Aurra Sing said.

"That was never part of the plan!" Boba said. "I just wanted to kill the Jedi that murdered my father!"

"Well, that will have to wait," Aurra said.

"Grow up . . . you'll get your revenge in time. Now get on board. We have to get out of here. Or you can go with your friends, who I'm going to jettison into the unknown."

Boba hesitated, then walked toward Aurra and the Trandoshan. He turned to seal the hatch behind him, trapping the cadets inside.

"I'm sorry," he said to Jax.

"Traitor," Jax replied.

Boba stepped away from the hatch, which muffled Whiplash and Hotshot's screams. Jax just stared at him.

"Do it," Aurra whispered in Boba's ear, the sound like the purr of a nexu.

"You'll regret this," Jax said.

Boba hit the release and the pod shot off into space. He watched it shrink to a bright dot. First he looked horrified. Then sad. Then his face showed no expression at all.

Anakin and Mace blasted away from the *Endurance* in their starfighters.

"We're caught in Vanqor's gravitational

pull," Kilian radioed to Anakin. "We're going to try and set her down on the surface."

"All right," the Jedi replied. "Once you're down, we'll get the rescue teams to your location—"

Another voice broke in.

"General Skywalker, this is Sergeant Crasher. It's the cadets, sir. I can't raise them on any channel, and their locator beacon's not active. Theirs is the only pod unaccounted for."

"Sounds like our saboteur may have gotten to the cadets," Mace said.

"We have to find that pod," Anakin said.

Later, aboard the pod, Jax stared at the inert control panels.

"I can't believe it," Hotshot kept saying. "A traitor. He was a traitor."

"We can't worry about that right now," Jax said. "We have to find a way to contact somebody."

"We already tried!" he shot back. "This pod is dead! We only have minimal life support!"

"Yeah?" demanded Whiplash. "And whose fault is that? That guy you defended left us for dead!"

"Stow it, Whiplash," Jax said. "We need to work together."

Whiplash's eyes were wild, and Jax waited for him to throw a punch. But then light filled the pod once again.

"They've come back to finish us off!" Hotshot wailed.

Jax peered through the hatch. "It's the Jedi!"

The two starfighters hung in space nearby, their astromechs' domes sticking out of their hulls. The two fighters dipped their wings reassuringly, a signal that help was on the way, then sped off.

CHAPTER 5

Mace and Anakin's starfighters raced over the surface of Vanqor. They were following a trail of smoking debris that ended at the twisted hulk of the *Endurance*.

"Set down behind the cruiser," Mace said. "We'll approach on foot."

On the planet's surface, Anakin climbed down from his cockpit while R2-D2 used a burst from his rockets to exit his socket in the hull. Surveying the gloomy landscape, R2 beeped worriedly.

"You're not kidding, little buddy," Anakin said. "I don't like the feel of this place, either."

Mace and droid R8-B7 went on ahead, avoiding chunks of smoking wreckage. Anakin and R2 followed.

"Ar-eight, start scanning the area for signs of life," Mace ordered. "And calculate an entry point to the cruiser."

As R2 followed the Jedi, something registered faintly on his sensors. He beeped an alarm and the Jedi turned. "A bit jittery, isn't he?" Mace asked.

"He must have seen something," Anakin said. "Right, Artoo?"

R2 chirped uncertainly.

"Come on," Mace said. "It looks like Ar-eight has found an entry point."

Mace and Anakin stared into the jagged hole in the *Endurance*'s hull, trying to make sense of the upside-down corridors and twisted metal inside. Wind had blown turquoise sand into the ruined interior.

R2 beeped sadly as his light picked out the body of a clone trooper. Mace knelt and gently rolled the body over.

"This man did not die in the crash," he said grimly, pointing to a scorch mark marring the white armor.

"The killer?" Anakin asked. "He beat us to the crash site? But why come here?"

"We know the assassins were after me," Mace said. "Perhaps they returned to look for my body."

R2's mournful chirp led them to another dead clone.

"We need to get to the bridge and find Admiral Kilian," Mace said. "Send the droids to scan for any survivors down here."

R2 bleated uncertainly, joining R8 as Anakin followed Mace to make the long climb up the turbolift shaft to the bridge.

"I know there's a lot of interference," Anakin said to R2. "Do your best. And be careful."

More clones lay in the wreckage of the bridge. But there was no sign of Kilian, Ponds, or the other officers.

"They must have been sucked into space when the cabin lost pressure," Mace said, activating his comlink to contact the Republic ships above. "Captain, there's no sign of any life down here. I'm afraid Admiral Kilian and

Commander Ponds are lost. Take the survivors back to the medical station. We'll meet you there."

At the other end of the turbolift shaft, R2's sensors picked up movement near the gash in the hull.

R2 beeped furiously at R8, but the other astromech refused to listen. Then R8 bumped into something. Their argument forgotten, the two astromechs aimed their visual sensors upward.

R8 had bumped into a gundark—two meters of muscle, teeth, and bad attitude.

The two droids raced off at top speed as the gundark screamed, bounding after them on its long legs. Just as the droids were about to escape the hangar, a second gundark leaped out from behind a chunk of debris and snatched up R8, who kicked his legs in panic.

R2 zapped the gundark with his electric prod, hoping the shock would stun it. But the beast batted the little droid across the hangar with a huge, clawed hand, leaving R2 lying on his side at the entrance to the turbolift. Before he could move, something skidded across the

deck. It was R8's dome, torn from his body. Now the gundarks were coming for R2.

On the wrecked bridge of the *Endurance*, Anakin noticed something in the debris.

"Is that a Mandalorian helmet?" he asked, puzzled. "What is that doing here?"

Mace looked from the battered steel helmet to the dead clones, then back.

"Clone cadets," he muttered to himself. "Jango Fett . . . Boba . . ."

Anakin knelt for a closer look at the helmet, then reached for it. Mace, still deep in thought, finally noticed what the younger Jedi was doing. His eyes widened.

"Anakin," Mace shouted. "NO!"

It was too late. As Anakin picked up the helmet, an enormous ball of flame rose from the gangway, the explosion engulfing both Jedi.

CHAPTER 6

Through his macrobinoculars, Boba Fett watched smoke and flames billow from the shattered bridge. Behind him, in front of the ship *Slave I*, stood Aurra Sing, the Trandoshan bounty hunter Bossk, and the fourth member of their crew, a scruffy-looking Klatooinian named Castas. Three hostages—Kilian, Ponds, and a clone navigation officer—lay bound and gagged nearby.

"Mace is dead," Aurra said. "Are you happy now?"

"I don't think he's dead," Boba said.

"I want to get off this planet now," Castas whined. "The place is crawling with gundarks, and besides, we've got these hostages to drag along with us now."

"I don't want to take hostages," Boba said. "I want Windu dead."

"Now, Boba," Aurra said. "This extra

baggage will fetch us a hefty sum from the Separatists. Along with your killing Windu, we're looking at a profit."

"It's a lot of trouble for not enough payout, if you ask me," Castas grumbled.

"You haven't even done anything!" Boba yelled. "I've taken all the risks!"

"Quiet, runt!" Castas yelled, moving to slap Boba. Before he could, he found himself staring down the barrel of Aurra's gun.

"I wouldn't do that," she said coldly.

Castas froze. Bossk just watched, his cold lizard eyes expressionless.

"Now relax," Aurra said. "Boba is right. To get paid we need proof of Windu's death. And if we killed Skywalker, we can ask for double."

That got Castas's attention.

"Double?" he asked.

"Yes, but we need proof."

Boba, Aurra, and Castas got on their speeder bikes, the engines roaring to life.

The explosion on the bridge had caused more debris to plunge from the upside-down deck of the hangar bay, crushing one gundark and scaring off the other. When the shaking stopped, R2 popped up from the wreckage. He tilted his body so he could look up the turbolift shaft. His Master was up there somewhere— and probably in trouble.

R2 rocketed up the shaft and into the ruined bridge. He kept beeping until finally he detected movement in the wreckage.

"Artoo," a voice called. "Over here."

Anakin was pinned down, with burns streaking his face. Mace lay nearby, also buried. He was unconscious.

"Good to see you, buddy," Anakin managed.

R2 tried to use his sensor arms to dig, but the debris began to shift and he stopped with a concerned warble.

"Careful, Artoo," Anakin said. "I need you to go back to the fighters and call the Jedi Temple for help. Okay?"

R2 beeped in agreement. He detected the sound of engines somewhere outside the cruiser. Anakin heard it, too.

"You're going to have to handle this one," Anakin said. "Cut them off somehow, then go get help. We'll hold out as long as we can. Go on, Artoo."

Boba, Aurra, and Castas stopped their speeder bikes alongside the *Endurance* and dismounted.

Their blasters were drawn.

"Come on," Boba said. "We've got to find Windu's body."

"Careful, Boba!" Aurra called.

A chunk of metal detached itself from the broken hull and crashed to the ground as Boba leaped out of the way.

"Yeah, careful," Castas said with a sneer. "I'd hate to only split the money three ways."

Boba scowled at Castas as the Klatooinian walked past him into the dark interior of the ship. Inside, they began their climb toward the bridge, dodging pieces of wreckage that came crashing down the sloping corridor.

"Look out!" Aurra yelled as a particularly large chunk of metal tumbled past them.

"This place is a death trap!" Castas said.

"When I hired you, I didn't realize that you were such a coward," Aurra said.

"Well, I don't want to be next," Castas said.

Aurra narrowed her eyes. Something wasn't right. Yes, the *Endurance*'s crash-landing had left it in pieces. But they shouldn't be dodging this much wreckage.

Ahead of them, R2 extended a computer interface arm toward the controls for one of the *Endurance*'s many blast doors. None of the chunks of metal he'd sent skidding down at the three hunters had stopped them, and they were getting closer. He told the controls to close the blast doors—but nothing happened.

The bounty hunters were close now. R2 tried again to override the computer problem. In a moment, they would see him.

The controls engaged and the blast door between R2 and the hunters slammed shut.

"Blast!" Aurra muttered.

"The door must have malfunctioned," Boba said. But Aurra's scowl told him she thought otherwise.

On the bridge, Anakin heard a labored cough. Mace had regained consciousness.

"My legs . . ." Mace said with a grunt. He freed his arms and tried to use the Force to shove the twisted metal off his lower body. There was an ominous groan from the pile.

"Careful," Anakin said. "I already tried that. You'll bring the whole place down on us."

"Well, how do we plan on getting ourselves out of this mess?" Mace demanded.

"Don't worry," Anakin said. "I already sent R2 back to the fighters to call for help."

Mace arched an eyebrow.

"I'm sure he has everything under control," Anakin insisted.

CHAPTER 7

"I'm just saying, I didn't know there'd be all this climbing involved," Castas complained as the hunters made their way up the turbolift shaft.

"Shut up already," Boba said.

That was enough for Aurra. "The next one who says anything will get a blaster bolt through the brain," she warned.

Above them, R2 removed a thermal detonator from a hiding place inside his chassis, triggered it, and dropped it into the shaft. He heard it bouncing, followed by a yell from one of the hunters.

BOOM!

The detonation sent the three hunters tumbling all the way back down to the hangar, pursued by billowing smoke and falling debris.

"That's it!" yelled Castas. "We're out of here! No one could survive this place!"

"A Jedi could!" Boba insisted.

"I hate to agree with Castas, but there is a better way to do this," Aurra said, activating a skinny antenna that rose from her head. "Bossk, fire up *Slave I*. We're going to blast what's left of this ship to pieces."

"I hate just sitting here," Anakin said.

"Calm yourself, Skywalker," Mace replied. "We'll soon see if the faith you put in that droid is worth it."

"I'm not worried about Artoo," Anakin said. "He always comes through. But I am worried about what he's up against. Do you know who is behind these attacks?"

Mace considered the question. He found himself staring across the bridge, where the scorched Mandalorian helmet was still sitting. As if it were watching them.

R2 had just jetted to the topside of Anakin's fighter when a gundark leaped onto the ship, rocking it back and forth. R2 squealed as the beast ripped the canopy off the cockpit and hurled it at the little droid, who dodged it with a flash of his rockets.

The monster's next blow knocked R2 to the ground and sent Anakin's fighter onto its side. Before R2 could get up, the gundark picked him up, holding him at arm's length.

Desperate, R2 fired a cable topped with a suction cup at the gundark, hitting it in the forehead. The surprised creature dropped R2, but he was now attached to the beast.

R2 dodged the gundark and attached his end of the cable to the hull of Anakin's fighter. The magnetic grapple held it fast. Then R2 reached an extender arm into the cockpit and hit the thrusters.

The ship's engines ignited, sending the fighter careening along the ground. The confused gundark watched the fighter as the cable stuck to its head unspooled. Then the beast was yanked off its feet and dragged behind the fighter.

R2 chuckled to himself.

Boba, Aurra, and Castas heard the blast as they were walking their speeder bikes up the ramp of *Slave I*.

"Scanners picked up an explosion near where the Jedi landed," said Bossk.

"Windu!" Boba said.

"Jam any communications off this planet," Aurra said. A minute later they took off, *Slave I* rising into the air.

R2 powered up Mace's fighter and lifted off. A warning buzzer sounded—his communications were being jammed!

R2 beeped worriedly, but within moments that was the least of his problems. A small spaceship came racing across the plain toward him, laser cannons firing.

Squealing in outrage, R2 raced Mace's fighter the length of the debris field, chased by the other ship. Bolts of energy ripped past him and into the cruiser's hull, tearing its engines apart and starting a fire.

"I don't like the sound of that," Anakin muttered.

Suddenly, Mace's fighter roared past the bridge, followed by another ship. Laser fire burst all around the fighter.

"I thought your astromech was supposed to call for help—not take off and leave us here," Mace said.

But Anakin was more worried about the droid than he was about Mace's opinion.

"C'mon, Artoo," he said. "I'm counting on you."

Above Vanqor, Mace's starfighter twisted and turned in a desperate attempt to evade *Slave I*'s laser blasts.

"Hold it steady!" Boba yelled at Bossk as he fired at the elusive fighter.

"You've knocked out his communications, but I can't keep up," the Trandoshan hissed.

R2's sensors located the two hyperspace rings. He accelerated toward them, dodging another volley of fire.

"If we can take out the rings, he'll be trapped," Aurra said.

"Which one?" Boba asked.

"Destroy them both!" snapped Aurra.

"You'll get one shot at this, kid," Bossk warned.

Boba narrowed his eyes, moving the crosshairs from one ring to the other, waiting to see which one the fighter's pilot would choose. Mace's fighter neared the left-hand ring. Then, suddenly, it rolled right, toward the other ring.

"I've got you, Windu!" Boba yelled, pulling the trigger.

The right-hand ring exploded. But R2 had continued to roll, banking under the deadly blasts. Now he rolled back, slotting Mace's fighter neatly into the socket of the left-hand ring. The fighter engaged its hyperdrive and a second later it was gone.

Boba's eyes widened.

"NO!" he yelled as he slumped in his seat.

"Well, there goes a fortune," growled

Castas. "Nice work, kid! Windu will be back here with a fleet. He'll hunt us down!"

"Don't count on it," Aurra said. "The Jedi don't carry grudges. But I have ways of motivating him."

She opened the door to the hold, where Kilian, Ponds, and the navigation officer lay on the floor.

"We'll make Windu come to us next time, on our terms," Aurra said. "Now let's get out of here."

CHAPTER 8

Mace used the Force to pull the battered Mandalorian helmet over to him.

Anakin looked over at Mace. "Whose helmet is that, anyway?" he asked.

"It belongs to a bounty hunter I killed on Geonosis," Mace replied solemnly. "By the name of Jango Fett."

"You mean the clone template?" Anakin asked the Jedi master.

Mace nodded grimly. "Yes, and strangely enough he had a son. Or at least a clone he regarded as a son. His name is Boba Fett. Boba was on Geonosis when his father died. He watched as I killed him."

"That would complicate things," Anakin replied thoughtfully.

Mace Windu stared at his own reflection in the visor.

"Indeed," he said.

Suddenly there was another loud explosion and the ship shook.

"It must be the main reactor," Mace said. "It's breaking down. And when it does—"

"—we'll be part of the landscape," Anakin said, knowing that they were in trouble.

In the Jedi Temple on Coruscant, Jedi Knights and Padawans had gathered for a strategy meeting. The Kel Dor Jedi Master Plo Koon gestured to a holographic map.

"We shall reinforce our fleet along the Hydian Way," Plo said. "This should prevent Grievous from—"

Suddenly the door opened and R2-D2 tumbled down the stairs.

"Artoo?" asked a surprised Ahsoka Tano, Anakin's Padawan. "What's wrong?"

R2 got to his feet and slammed into Plo Koon's astromech R7-D4, who was controlling the holo-table. An upset R7 bumped him back. As the Jedi watched in disbelief, the two droids shoved each other, beeping and whistling angrily.

"Ahsoka, you know this droid?" Plo asked the young Togruta.

"It's Anakin's droid, Artoo Detoo."

Plo nodded. "Well then, Artoo, deliver the message you so obviously need to communicate."

A moment later, all the Jedi were staring at a hologram of the trapped Anakin Skywalker.

"Prepare my ship," Plo said. "We shall leave immediately."

"Your astromech has been gone too long," Mace said. "He must have failed to deliver your message."

"Artoo will come through," Anakin insisted. "I know it."

"You put too much trust in that droid," Mace said.

The two breathed deeply and began to focus, so as to summon the Force. The bridge trembled and began to collapse with a groan of metal. But Anakin heard another sound—the hum of Republic gunships!

"There!" Ahsoka said from the gunship, pointing down at the wreckage of the *Endurance*. "In the bridge!"

R2 beeped and whistled.

"Ahsoka, hold the ship steady," Plo said.

The gunship hovered next to the bridge. Commander Wolffe and his men fired cables at the shaky structure as Plo and Ahsoka used the Force to keep the bridge intact.

"We're losing it, sir!" yelled a clone pilot.

A huge explosion shook the bridge and sent the gunship fluttering away before the pilot could get it back under control. Commander Wolffe and another clone trooper jumped to the bridge and pulled the trapped Jedi free as it began to break apart. Holding Anakin and Mace tightly, the troopers jumped back, guided into the gunship by Ahsoka and Plo.

The explosion kicked the gunship sideways as Plo yelled, "Cut the lines! Go!"

As the gunship raced away, a final explosion erupted, marking the end of the *Endurance*.

CHAPTER 9

On Coruscant, Anakin and Mace were resting in the Jedi Temple's medcenter. Mace read from a datapad while Anakin stared out the window at the endless river of speeder traffic in the sky.

"So what are you planning to do with this son of Jango Fett?" Anakin asked.

Mace didn't look up. "I am not planning to do anything."

"That kid destroyed an entire cruiser trying to get you," Anakin said. "And you're just going to let it go?"

"Is there something else I should be doing, Skywalker?" Mace asked.

"How about trying to track him down?" Anakin replied.

That, finally, got Mace to look at him.

"So I should behave as this child does?" he asked. "I should seek revenge?"

"Not revenge, Master," Anakin added. "A preemptive strike! He's going to kill you!"

"In case you hadn't noticed, we are fighting a war," Mace replied.

Anakin opened his mouth to argue further, but the door slid open. Plo Koon and Ahsoka Tano came in.

"We have a situation," Plo said, turning on the room's holoprojector and dimming the lights with a wave of his hand. "We received a transmission from the bounty hunters. They apparently took hostages."

A hologram flickered to life, showing Aurra and Boba with their blasters aimed at three hostages.

"Mace Windu!" said Boba. "You were lucky to escape. Your friends here were not so fortunate."

Boba raised his weapon and faced the prisoners. The young bounty hunter looked uncertain—scared, even.

"Until you face Boba," Aurra warned, "these men will not be safe."

"Boba, do it," Aurra growled.

Boba looked at Ponds, who calmly looked back. He hesitated.

"Boba!" Aurra barked.

Ahsoka, Anakin, and Plo winced at the crack of blaster fire. Mace watched without expression. Smoke curled from the barrel of Aurra Sing's blaster.

"Only two to go, Windu," she said. "Come and find us. We'll be waiting!"

The hologram winked out and the shades came up, leaving the Jedi standing silently in bright sunlight.

"I'll go," Mace said.

"I thought you had bigger concerns," Anakin said, drawing a sharp look from the older Jedi.

"That was before we knew hostages were involved," Mace answered.

"You are not ready to travel, and your presence would only aggravate the boy," replied Plo. "I will go, and take Padawan Tano with me."

CHAPTER 10

Bossk and Castas were sitting in the cockpit when Boba came in and flung himself into an empty chair. Aurra was right behind him.

"It should only be a matter of time until they track us down," she said with satisfaction.

Castas shifted uncomfortably in his seat.

"Something on your mind, Castas?" Aurra asked.

"Yeah, I got something to say," the bounty hunter said. "We're in over our heads."

"You signed on to kill Jedi," Aurra said. "Well, this is how it's done."

"You said the Separatists would pay well if we killed Windu," Castas objected. "That kid destroyed an entire cruiser, and now we're taking hostages. That was not part of the plan."

"I never took you for a coward, Castas," Aurra said. "What about you, Bossk? You feel the same?"

"I'm still in," the Trandoshan hissed. "I got a lot riding on this. And I need the cash."

"Not me," Castas said. "I'm out."

"You're in luck," Aurra said. "I was planning on making a stop. You can drag your worthless carcass off this ship when we land."

"Where are we headed?" Boba asked.

"We're going to visit an old friend," Aurra said. "Maybe he can replace Castas. Set course for Florrum."

A Jedi speeder zoomed through the air between Coruscant's giant skyscrapers, then flew over an open area marked by low buildings.

"Master Plo, I don't understand," Ahsoka said. "Shouldn't we be heading for the last place we knew Boba Fett was spotted?"

"Why head to the one place we know he is not?" the Kel Dor Jedi replied. "The second hunter in the hologram was Aurra Sing."

"Another bounty hunter?" Ahsoka asked. "Like his father, Jango Fett?"

"Yes," Plo said. "It seems this boy found himself in the care of at least one of Jango's associates."

"So we're looking for friends of Jango Fett, or places where they hang out?" Ahsoka Tano asked the Jedi master.

Plo nodded behind his breath mask. "And to do that, we must go to the lower levels—the underworld."

The speeder banked sharply and passed through a huge, circular hole in the cityscape, one of the giant passageways that brought air and light to the lower levels.

"The data on Jango Fett suggested he frequented this area," Plo said. "We must be cautious."

On Florrum, the leathery Weequay pirate Hondo Ohnaka strode out of his fortress, guards falling in on either side of him. Aurra Sing was walking down *Slave I*'s ramp.

Hondo grinned. "My dear, you never were good at asking for permission to land."

"I never ask for permission to do anything, my darling," Aurra said. She kissed Hondo on the lips.

"Yes," Hondo said, wiping his mouth. "I remember."

He looked at the boy with Aurra and raised an eyebrow.

"He's Jango's son," Aurra said.

"Ahh, yes. Sorry about your father," the Weequay pirate said. "He was a friend—and an honorable man."

Boba nodded, then looked at his feet.

"And that's Castas," Aurra said. "But he's getting off here."

"Couldn't handle her, could you?" Hondo asked with a smirk. "Well, don't be ashamed—you're not the first man to bail out from under her command."

"He's speaking from experience," Aurra said.

Hondo grinned. "Oh! You're a dangerous woman! Yes, ha-ha! Very dangerous. Come, come! Let's go inside where we can discuss business over a drink."

The bar was crowded with pirates of all shapes and sizes. Boba spotted Weequay, Nikto, Ithorians, and scruffy humans. As the bartender slid drinks to Hondo and his guests, Castas went to use a holo-transmitter across the room.

Boba reached for a mug when Aurra shook her head no at him. As Boba scowled, the chalk white bounty hunter saw Castas speaking into the holo-transmitter and frowned. The antenna in her skull quietly rose as she continued to talk to Hondo.

"I'm stuck out here on Florrum," she heard Castas say, his voice amplified by her antenna.

"I warned you," the voice on the other end of the line said. "Working with Aurra Sing is bad business."

"This job's gone south," Castas said. "Like every job I do with that hag!"

The bartender poured two new drinks. Hondo took one and Boba reached for the other.

"No, Boba," Aurra said.

"So, Boba, what's it like working with Aurra?" Hondo asked. "Must be quite an adventure. She's basically like your mother— something like that, yes?"

Aurra was still using her antenna to eavesdrop on Castas.

"I have some information," Castas said. "Information that's worth something to the right people."

Aurra's eyes narrowed.

"You know, Aurra and I go back a long way," Hondo told Boba. "In fact, we both knew your father, but you probably know that."

Castas leaned closer to the holo-transmitter. Whoever he was talking to sounded interested.

"Remember, Aurra, that job we pulled?" Hondo asked.

"Hmm? Yes, excuse me," Aurra replied as she spun around and pulled out her blaster. "Castas!"

Castas turned to find himself staring at the business end of Aurra's blaster. It was the last thing he ever saw.

CHAPTER 11

The Jedi speeder touched down in an alley. Plo and Ahsoka stepped out, ponchos covering their Jedi robes. Ahead of them, an orange neon sign flickered in the gloom.

"Well, I hope we have better luck here," Ahsoka said. "This is the fifth scum-bucket drinking hole we've been to."

"Yes, and this time try to be more subtle," Plo said.

"What do you mean?" Ahsoka asked.

"You have adopted many of your Master's ways, including a lack of subtlety," Plo answered. "Try to blend in. Listen."

Inside the bar, raucous music was playing and ruffians of various species filled the room.

"Have a look around," Plo told Ahsoka, heading for the counter. Ahsoka looked sadly at the Twi'lek dancing girl and walked slowly through the bar. She took a deep breath and closed her eyes, using the Force to help her overhear individual speakers.

Drink, drink, another drink.

She's so purrrdy. Look at her twirling around.

This war is killing me—my whole business has gone under. Ah, gimme another round.

Florrum? A buddy of mine was just murdered on Florrum.

Ahsoka raised her eyebrows and listened more closely.

"Yeah, yeah, he was working a big job," said a Nautolan pirate sitting with a gang of Weequay. "At least that's what he said."

Ahsoka edged closer.

"He was telling me he had some valuable information," the pirate continued. "And then—*BOOM!* She shot him. It must have been some good dirt."

"So, Fong Do, what's her name?" another thug asked. "I hope it's not who I think it is."

"He was working with Aurra Sing," Fong Do replied. "She's bad news."

Ahsoka's eyes widened.

"Eh, that's her, all right," the other thug said. "She's the boss's ex-girlfriend. There's always trouble when she shows up."

Suddenly the thug noticed Ahsoka eavesdropping, grabbed her, and put her in a headlock.

"Find something interesting, kid?" he asked.

Ahsoka twisted away and elbowed him hard in the gut. The music stopped. Ahsoka reached for her lightsaber, only to find blasters pointing at her from all sides.

"What's this?" Fong Do demanded. "What are you reaching for?"

Suddenly Ahsoka heard the most wonderful sound she'd ever heard—the snap-hiss of another lightsaber igniting. Heads turned to see Plo standing by the bar, poncho thrown to one side to reveal his Jedi robes, his blue lightsaber in one hand.

The thug let go and Ahsoka took her place by Plo's side, drawing her own lightsaber.

"You can't take us all, Jedi!" Fong Do yelled to them.

"Would you like to try and prove your theory?" Plo asked quietly.

"Nobody's shooting up my place today!" the bartender yelled.

Ahsoka looked at the crowd and the blasters still aimed at them.

"He's right," she said to the crowd. "Drinks on the house!"

The thugs began to cheer.

"Now wait a minute!" the bartender protested, but the crowd was already pushing forward. In the chaos, Ahsoka and Plo stepped outside.

"I was being subtle!" Ahsoka said.

"Interesting result," Plo said.

"But, Master, you were right," Ahsoka said. "I heard about a murder. A murder Aurra Sing recently committed. On Florrum."

"Well done, little 'Soka," Plo said. "We are off to Florrum."

On Florrum, Hondo and his guards were outside waiting when the Jedi shuttle touched down on the planet's surface. Down the ramp walked Plo Koon and Ahsoka.

"Hello, hello—and welcome to Florrum!" Hondo said, escorting the two Jedi toward a building.

"I should assume you are walking us into a trap?" Plo asked.

"They're in there, waiting inside the bar," Hondo said. "I don't know what she has planned for you."

"The reason you are telling us is?" Plo Koon added.

"I want you to know that I am not involved in this," Hondo said.

Plo nodded to the younger Jedi, indicating she should wait by the door.

"Remember, patience," he said.

CHAPTER 12

Plo found Aurra in the dark, empty bar at a table illuminated by a single light. He sat down across from her.

"Bad move, Jedi," the bounty hunter said. "This will cost you."

Boba stepped out of the shadows, his blaster aimed at the back of Plo's head.

"I wanted Windu," he said. "What are you doing here?"

Plo turned his head just enough to acknowledge Boba's presence. Then he looked back at Aurra.

"We can do this the difficult way or the simple way," the Jedi said. "The choice is yours."

The antenna rose from Aurra's head.

"Bossk, can you hear me?" she said. "Execute the hostages if I give the word."

"Unwise," Plo said. "You have already lost and you don't even know it."

"I am prepared to kill you, the hostages, whatever it takes to get what Boba wants," Aurra said.

"It sounds more like what *you* want," Plo replied.

Suddenly Ahsoka appeared behind Aurra. In a flash she ignited her lightsaber, slashed off Aurra's antenna and held the bright blade at her throat.

Boba moved in closer to Plo.

"Don't!" Ahsoka warned Boba, her lightsaber held at Aurra's throat. It was a standoff.

"Let her go," Boba said, looking frightened.

"No chance," Ahsoka replied.

"She won't do it, Boba," Aurra said. "She's not like you."

"She's right," Ahsoka said. "I'm not a murderer."

Boba hesitated.

"I'm not a murderer," he said. "But I want justice!"

"We *are* justice," Plo said.

"Don't listen to them!" Aurra said.

"No one will be harmed if you come quietly," Plo said.

Boba looked at Aurra.

"I can't let you die," he said miserably.

"You won't have to," she said. And then she winked at Boba.

Suddenly Aurra was moving—far more quickly than Ahsoka had expected. Boba fired at Ahsoka, who blocked the bolt with her lightsaber, while deadly darts zipped out from under the table at Plo. Quicker than the eye could follow, the Kel Dor flipped the table to block the darts and knocked Boba backward with an elbow that sent his blaster spinning across the floor.

Aurra drew her pistols and fired a volley of shots at Ahsoka, forcing her back. Plo used the Force to shove the table into the path of the bolts and ignited his own lightsaber. One swing and Aurra's pistols were sliced in half, leaving her defenseless.

"It's over," Plo said. "Surrender."

Aurra tossed a thermal detonator onto the floor. The device was already chiming as its timer counted down. The blast sent all four of them flying through the air.

Aurra came to her senses near the door. Both Jedi were getting up. Boba was still lying on the floor.

"Boba, hurry!" she cried.

Boba tried to get up, but Plo stretched out his hand. Using the Force, the Jedi pulled Boba into his grip. Aurra ran for it, with Ahsoka in pursuit.

"Aurra, help!" yelled Boba. "Don't leave me!"

"The hostages," Plo said. "Where are they? Boba, if you don't tell me where those men are, they are going to die. Innocent men!"

"She left me," Boba said in despair.

Aurra ran out into the Florrum night, past Hondo and his pirates. One aimed his blaster at her, but a signal from Hondo stopped him. She leaped onto a speeder bike and roared off into the darkness.

A moment later, Ahsoka rushed out after her. Again the pirate lifted his gun—and again Hondo stopped him. Ahsoka zoomed away on a second bike.

"If we don't get involved, we'll come out ahead on this one," Hondo said. "Trust me."

Plo emerged from the compound, a handcuffed Boba beside him.

"He will not reveal the location of the hostages," Plo said to Hondo. "I thought you might talk some sense into him."

Hondo looked at Boba and saw the sorrow on his face.

"Tell the Jedi what he wants to know, Boba," he said, almost gently.

"Why should I help anybody?" Boba demanded. "I've got no one!"

"It is the honorable thing to do," Hondo replied. "It's what your father would have wanted."

Bossk waited with the hostages for further orders. Now he decided he'd waited long enough.

"Time's up," he hissed, pointing his rifle at Admiral Kilian and the clone officer.

Suddenly a speeder bike shot out of the darkness, its driver firing wildly at Bossk. He dove for cover, dropping his rifle. Ahsoka leaped from the bike and cut the hostages loose.

Another bike roared up. Aurra jumped off and her riderless bike smashed into Ahsoka's at top speed. Both exploded. Before anyone could react, the bounty hunter had raced aboard *Slave I* and begun powering up its engines.

Ahsoka ran after Aurra. Bossk drew his pistol, then stopped. A rifle was aimed at his head, he realized—his own rifle, the one he had dropped. Holding it was Kilian.

"Don't move," he said.

Bossk dropped the gun and raised his hands.

As *Slave I* rose into the sky and tilted into flight position, Ahsoka jumped onto one of its square wings. Aurra saw her and banked the ship sharply, trying to knock the Padawan off. Ahsoka slashed at the wing with her lightsaber, cutting off a stabilizer.

Slave I began to spin. Aurra looked frantic. Ahsoka leaped off as the ship spiraled out of control. It hit the ground somewhere beyond the ridge and an explosion lit up the night.

On Coruscant, Mace Windu and Anakin Skywalker were waiting when Plo and Ahsoka returned in the Jedi shuttle. Down the ramp they came, along with a handcuffed Boba and Bossk and the two freed hostages.

Boba saw Mace waiting on the landing platform.

"Next time I won't let so many innocents get in the way," he said, and then spat at Mace. "Next time it will be just you and me."

The two stood there, staring into each other's eyes. Then, finally, Mace spoke.

"There won't be a next time," he said.

Plo and Ahsoka led Boba away. Behind them on the platform, Mace kept watching the young bounty hunter, saying nothing. He stood that way for a long time.